No Roses for
HARRY!

No Roses for
HARRY!

Gene Zion

Illustrated by Margaret Bloy Graham

Mini Treasures
RED FOX

NO ROSES FOR HARRY
A RED FOX BOOK 0099 281767

First published in Great Britain by The Bodley Head Children's Books 1961
an imprint of Random House Children's Books

First Red Fox Mini Treasures edition published 1999
This Red Fox Mini Treasures edition published 2003

3 5 7 9 10 8 6 4

Text copyright © Eugene Zion 1958
Illustrations copyright © Margaret Bloy Graham 1958

Papers used by Random House Children's Books are natural, recyclable products made
from wood grown in sustainable forests. The manufacturing processes conform to the
environmental regulations of the country of origin.

Red Fox Books are published by Random House Children's Books,
61-63 Uxbridge Road, London W5 5SA,
a division of The Random House Group Ltd,
in Australia by Random House Australia (Pty) Ltd,
20 Alfred Street, Milsons Point, Sydney, NSW 2061, Australia,
in New Zealand by Random House New Zealand Ltd,
18 Poland Road, Glenfield, Auckland 10, New Zealand,
and in South Africa by Random House (Pty) Ltd,
Endulini, 5A Jubilee Road, Parktown 2193, South Africa

THE RANDOM HOUSE GROUP Limited Reg. No. 954009
www.kidsatrandomhouse.co.uk

A CIP catalogue record for this book is available from the British Library.

Printed in China

Harry was a white dog with black spots.
On his birthday, he got a present from
Grandma.
It was a woollen sweater with roses on it.
Harry didn't like it the moment he saw it.
He didn't like the roses.

When he tried it on, he felt cosy and snug.
But he still didn't like the roses.
He thought it was the silliest sweater
he'd ever seen.

The next day when Harry went into town
with the children, he wore his new sweater.
When people saw it, they laughed.
When dogs saw it, they barked.
Harry made up his mind then and there
to lose Grandma's present.

When they went into a big store to shop,
the children took off his sweater and let him
carry it. This was just what Harry wanted.

First he tried to lose it in the pet department –

but a man found it and gave it back.

Then he tried to lose it in the
grocery department –

but a lady found it and gave it back.

He tried to lose it in the flower department –

but a little boy found it and gave it back.

The children didn't let Harry carry
it any more. They made him wear it.
As they started home, Harry was
beginning to think he'd never lose it.

When he got home, his friends were
waiting to play with him. But Harry didn't
feel like playing so they left him alone.

As he sat wondering what to do, Harry
noticed a loose stitch in his sweater.
He pulled at the wool – just a little at first –
then a bit more – and a little bit more.
Harry didn't know it, but a bird was watching.

In a minute, Harry had pulled out
quite a long piece of the wool.
The end of it lay on the grass behind him.
Suddenly the bird flew down.

Quick as a flash she took the end of the
wool in her beak and flew away with it!
It all happened before Harry could
even blink.

The sweater began to disappear right before Harry's eyes. First one leg – then the neck –

then the other leg – then the back – and finally

the whole thing was just one long, long
piece of wool flying off into the sky.
The sweater was gone! Harry could
hardly believe it.

He barked and jumped with joy!
Then he ran out of the garden.

He ran down the street barking thank you
to the bird over and over again.

The bird and wool were just a tiny speck in the sky, but Harry kept following them.

He came home thirsty and tired, and was having a drink in the kitchen when the children ran in.
"We've got a letter from Grandma!" said one.
"She's coming to visit us!" shouted the other.
Harry thought of the sweater and his tail drooped.

Before Grandma came, the family looked
everywhere for the sweater. They wanted
her to see how nice Harry looked in it.
Of course they couldn't find it. Only Harry
knew why.

When Grandma arrived, Harry ran
to her with his leash. Then he sat up
and begged.
"All right, Harry," said Grandma.
"After I've had my lunch and a nap,
we'll go for a walk."

That afternoon, Harry and Grandma
and the children started off on their
walk. Harry barked happily and pulled
towards the park.

When they got to the park, Harry pulled
harder. The children let him off his leash
and he ran on ahead. He seemed to be
looking for something.

All at once, he stopped under a big tree.
He looked up and began to bark and
wag his tail. Grandma and the children
came running.

They got to the tree and looked up too.
Suddenly one of the children said, "I see a <u>nest</u>!"
"It's made of <u>wool</u>!" said the other,
"and it's the <u>very</u> <u>same</u> <u>colour</u> as—"
"<u>Harry's</u> <u>sweater</u>!" they shouted together.

"It <u>is</u> Harry's sweater!" exclaimed Grandma.
Just then a bird looked out of the nest.
"Look! Grandma, look!" shouted the children.
"Harry gave his sweater to a bird!"
"I wonder how he did that!" said Grandma.
The bird sang and Harry wagged his tail
even harder.

At Christmas, Harry got a present
from Grandma.
It was a <u>new</u> sweater!
Harry liked this one very much.
When he tried it on, he felt as cosy
and snug as the bird in the nest.
But best of all – it was white with
black spots!